APR -- 2002

Eileen Spinelli

The Giggle and Cry Book

Illustrated by Lisa Atherton

Stemmer House

PUBLISHERS, INC.

Owings Mills, Maryland

Text copyright © 1981 by Eileen Spinelli
Illustrations copyright © 1981 by Lisa Atherton

Inquiries should be directed to
Stemmer House Publishers, Inc.
2627 Caves Road
Owings Mills, Maryland 21117

Published simultaneously in Canada by Houghton Mifflin Company, Ltd.,
Markham, Ontario

A Barbara Holdridge book
Printed and bound in the United States of America
First Edition

Library of Congress Cataloging in Publication Data
Spinelli, Eileen.
  The giggle and cry book.
  Summary: Rhyming text lists things that make
you laugh and cry.
  [1. Laughing—Fiction. 2. Crying—Fiction.
3. Stories in rhyme] I. Atherton, Lisa.
II. Title.
PZ8.3.S759Gi   [E]   81-5654
ISBN 0-916144-88-7   AACR2

To
My daughter, Lana
and
My niece, Chrissie Hill

What makes me giggle?
A moose with a wiggle.

Ten tickled toes,
One blowing nose.

A bubble, a belly,
A faceful of jelly.

Pogo-sticking,
And puppies licking.

An acorn kerplunking,
Fall apple-dunking.

A cuckooing clock,
A hole in my sock.

Clowns colliding,
Pony riding.

Spaghetti slurping,
Babies burping.

Mudpies, monkeys,
Hats on donkeys.

Squirting rings,
Fizzy things.

Two front teeth missing,
Hugging and kissing.

A fat, dancing bear,
Long red underwear.

Bright chiming bells,
Fast carousels.

Toys that jiggle,
Worms that squiggle . . .

What makes you giggle?

What makes me cry?
Sand in my eye.

Bruises and bumps,
Oatmeal with lumps.

Sniffles and sneezing,
Bullies and teasing.

Homeless kittens,
Misplaced mittens.

Broken blue wagons,
Nightmares with dragons.

Onions chopping,
Ice cream plopping.

Losing Dad's pliers,
Kites caught in wires.

Hot soup spilling,
Ghost tales chilling.

My cupcake squashed,
My hair getting washed.

A scolding from Mother,
A fight with my brother.

Getting lost in the park,
Sometimes . . . the dark.

A dull rainy day,
Friends moving away.

Shoes that won't tie,
Waving goodbye . . .

What makes you cry?

NO MATTER WHAT . . .
After we cry and grumble and pout
And let all our sniffly sad feelings out,
Let's visit again that moose with a wiggle,
And have ourselves
        another
                good
                        giggle!

Designed by Barbara Holdridge
Composed by Speed Graphics Corporation, Reisterstown, Maryland in
Benguiat Medium and Palatino, with Torino Flair display composed by
Service Composition Company, Baltimore, Maryland
Color separation by Capper, Inc. and printed by
Federated Lithographers, Providence, Rhode Island on 80-lb. Glatco Matte
Hardbound by Delmar Printing Company, Charlotte, North Carolina